Jamaican Village

John and Penny Hubley

Adam and Charles Black · London

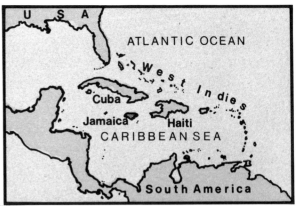

This is Dorothy Samuels. She lives in Cascade, a village near Montego Bay, on the north coast of Jamaica.

Jamaica is one of a group of islands in the Caribbean Sea. The islands were discovered by Christopher Columbus in 1492, when he was trying to sail round the world. They are called the West Indies because when Columbus reached the islands, he thought he had discovered India.

When Columbus arrived, a group of people called the Arawaks were living in Jamaica. They called their island 'Xaymaca', which means 'Land of Woods and Water'. The name Jamaica comes from this Arawak word.

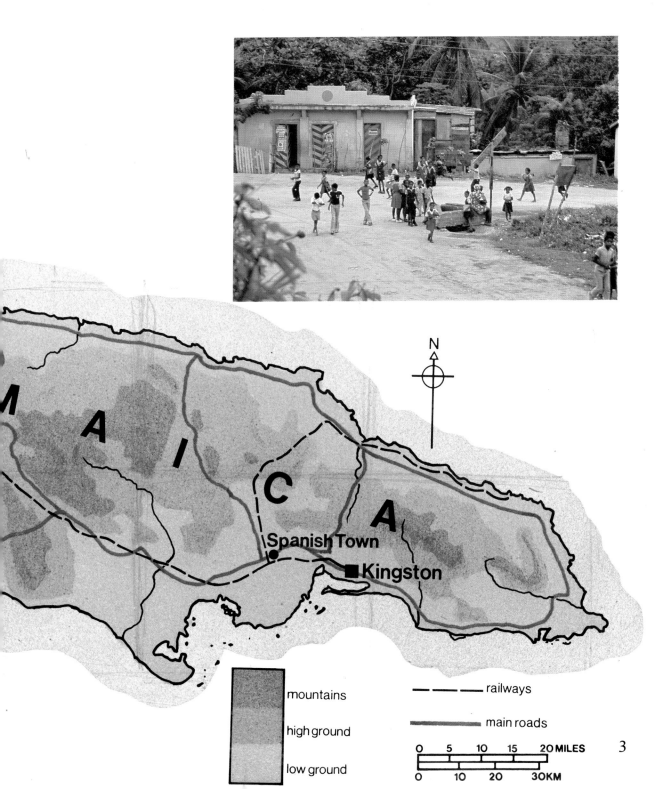

N

		mountains
		high ground
		low ground

- - - - railways

main roads

| 0 | 5 | 10 | 15 | 20 MILES |
| 0 | 10 | 20 | 30KM |

M A I C A

Spanish Town

Kingston

3

Dorothy is ten years old. She lives with her parents, her sister and her brother. Their house is made of brightly painted wood and has a corrugated iron roof.

At the front of the house, there is a big shady veranda. Dorothy and her family often sit on the veranda to keep cool. In Jamaica, the weather is hot all year round, so Dorothy's house is built on pillars, to catch the breeze. From the veranda, you can see coconut, orange and breadfruit trees which grow in the garden.

Outside the house, there is a water tap. In the past, people from the village had to collect water from the streams and carry it back home. But now, water is piped to every house in the village.

Dorothy's sister is a college student in Kingston, the capital city of Jamaica. This month she's on holiday, so she has come home to see her family.

Although she's on holiday, Dorothy's sister has to study. She does her work in the living room. The room is decorated with pictures and cards. Some of the cards come from relatives who live in London.

Dorothy's sister helps to cook lunch. The family has a gas stove. They buy the gas in large metal containers. Some Jamaican families cook on paraffin stoves or wood fires.

5

Cascade is a small village. About two thousand
people live there. In the past, the village was larger
and a big market was held there every week. Now,
more people work in the towns and Cascade is not
as busy as it used to be.

There are five grocery shops in the village which
sell things like tinned food, biscuits, soft drinks and
soap. Sometimes the villagers bring vegetables and
fruit from their gardens for the shopkeeper to sell.

The small village library is open every afternoon.
After school has finished, children often call in to
read or borrow books.

Next to the library is a health clinic where mothers bring their babies to be examined by the nurse. There is also a post office and a bank in the village.

Dorothy and her family go to church on Sundays. Dorothy goes to the Sunday school. Before the service starts, the grown-ups like to listen to the children singing.

Dorothy goes to the village school. The school is in a big modern building and children from all the nearby villages have lessons there.

Dorothy started school when she was five years old. Next year, when she is eleven, she will take an important examination. If she passes the exam, she will go to the high school in Montego Bay. Dorothy likes school. She wants to go to college when she is older, like her sister does.

School children in Jamaica wear uniforms. Dorothy's uniform is blue, but each school has a different uniform.

Some of the girls in Dorothy's school have their hair plaited in fancy styles. This keeps them cool and looks very smart. The girls get their mothers or friends to plait their hair. Some of the hair styles can take hours to do.

Dorothy's elder brother, Martin, also goes to the village school. After school, he earns some pocket money by running errands for people in the village. He carries goods in a wooden cart which he has made. The cart is guided by a steering wheel and has lights and bumpers, like a big lorry.

Most of the people in Cascade are farmers. The Samuels have their own farm which is run by Dorothy's grandfather. One of the most important crops is the yam plant. This is a tall vine which has to be held up by a cane. You can't eat the leaves of the yam plant. The part that you can eat grows under the ground.

Before the yams can be planted, the farmworkers have to prepare the fields. First, they dig up the fields and make mounds of earth. Then they plant one yam into each mound, using a tool called a hoe.

This is hard work, so everyone stops for an hour's rest at lunchtime. Each worker is given a daily wage and a cooked mid-day meal.

Dorothy's grandfather checks the vines every day to make sure that they are healthy. When the yams are ready for harvesting, the viñes die down. Then the yams are dug up from the earth.

Most of the farms in Cascade are small – less than ten acres. But the farmers grow all kinds of different crops.

The Samuels family grows coconuts, bananas, cocoa, potatoes, oranges, avocado pears and other kinds of fruit and vegetables, as well as yams.

Dorothy's family eats some of the food which grows on their farm. They store most of the yams and potatoes to eat in the months after harvest. The rest of the fruit and vegetables are sold to people in the village, or at the market in Montego Bay.

Dorothy's mum makes cocoa from her own cocoa beans. When the cocoa pods are ripe, they are cut down. Then the beans are taken out of the pods and dried in the sun. Most of the beans are sold to a factory that makes cocoa powder and chocolate.

The Samuels are very proud of their cows because they have had strong, healthy calves. The calves are kept for about a year and then sold to a local butcher. The cows have to be tied up, or they would eat all the crops! There is hardly any fresh milk in Jamaica. Most people have to use tinned or powdered milk. But the Samuels family can drink fresh milk from their own cows.

Dorothy's uncle lives on a nearby farm. He keeps goats for their milk and pigs and chickens for meat. People from the surrounding villages often come to his farm to buy from him. The animals are weighed to work out the price. Dorothy's uncle also keeps bees and sells the honey they make.

Sometimes, Dorothy's family have lunch at her uncle's farm. Dorothy's favourite Jamaican dish is Jerk Pork. The pork is spiced and cooked slowly on a fire of green wood. The smoky fire gives the meat its special taste.

Jerk Pork was first cooked over two hundred years ago. At that time, the sailors who came to Jamaica had spent many weeks at sea, eating ship's rations. They wanted fresh food, so they caught wild pigs to eat. As there was no dry firewood, they had to cut down trees and cook the pork on green wood.

Jamaica is famous for its sugar. Three quarters of the sugar made there is taken to Britain. But the tall sugar canes look very different from the sugar we use.

Dorothy's dad works on a sugar farm, or plantation. At harvest time he cuts down the sugar cane with a tool called a cutlass. This tool has a big sharp blade and is used for pruning and digging as well as harvesting.

Before the cane is harvested, it is burnt to remove the dry leaves. This makes it easier to cut. It's still very hard work and the men get covered in black ash.

When the cane has been cut, it's picked up by a grabbing machine, loaded into waggons and taken to the sugar factory. At the factory, the cane is crushed to release the sweet juice inside. This juice is turned into light brown sugar. Some of the sugar is made into rum at the factory.

The sugar cane is harvested between January and August. During the rest of the year, the workers plant more sugar and clean and repair the machines in the factory.

Every Saturday there is a big market in Montego Bay. Dorothy's mother and grandmother go to the market very early in the morning. They sell fruit and vegetables from the family farm.

The weekly market is colourful and busy. Dorothy's mother and grandmother put out their fruit and vegetables in the same place every week. They know all the other traders and everyone chats as they work. Sometimes Dorothy comes too. When she is older, she wants to help at the market.

The traders at the market are all women. Jamaicans have a special name for women traders. They call them 'higglers'.

People from Montego Bay and the nearby villages come to the market every week. They meet their friends and buy all kinds of different vegetables and fruits.

Ackee is one of the most popular kinds of fruit at the market. It is the national fruit of Jamaica. Ackee grows on trees and is poisonous until it splits open. You can't eat the black seeds inside the fruit, but the yellow flesh is delicious. It tastes like a mixture of chestnuts and scrambled eggs. Ackee and saltfish is the Jamaican national dish.

1 **Green banana**
2 **Yam**
3 **Sweet potatoes**
4 **Plantain**
5 **Sugar cane**
6 **Spinach**
7 **Limes**
8 **Coconut**
9 **Turnips**
10 **Squash**
11 **Cabbage**
12 **Avocado pear**
13 **Tomatoes**
14 **Pawpaw**
15 **Carrots**

Montego Bay is a busy town. It has lots of shops, offices, banks, cinemas and restaurants, as well as the weekly market. People from Dorothy's village often go to the town. Usually they go by bus, along the twisting road through the hills. Some people make the trip every day to go to work or school.

The shops in Cascade village are small, so the villagers sometimes go shopping in Montego Bay. They can buy things like clothes, shoes, furniture and books there. The supermarkets in the town sell lots of different kinds of food which you can't buy in Cascade.

There is no doctor in Cascade. People who are ill have to go to the hospital in Montego Bay.

Dorothy enjoys going on trips to Montego Bay. When her mum has finished work at the market, they look round the big shops. As a special treat, Dorothy sometimes has an ice cream or sky juice. Sky juice is her favourite. It's made of ice and sweet fruit juice and comes in a plastic bag or cup.

Lots of people from other countries come to
Jamaica for their holidays. They like the sunshine,
beaches and beautiful mountains. Most of them
come by aeroplane and stay in the big hotels
near the sea.

Many Jamaicans work in the offices, kitchens and restaurants of these hotels. Some of the people from Dorothy's village work as waiters and cooks.

Hardly any tourists go to Cascade. But, in Montego Bay, Dorothy often sees the tourists looking for presents to take home. They buy straw hats, baskets, T-shirts and wooden carvings. They can even see some of the souvenirs being made.

Dorothy knows about the history of her country. After Columbus discovered Jamaica, people from Europe went to live there. They were farmers and grew sugar to send to Britain. These farmers needed workers for their plantations, so they brought people from Africa to work on the farms. The farmers owned the slaves and did not pay them for working.

The slaves wanted to be free. Many of them ran away or tried to fight for their freedom. Some Europeans said that the slaves should be free. Others wanted to keep their slaves. They argued about this for many years. Then, in 1834, a law was passed freeing all slaves.

Some of the sugar farmers became very wealthy and built grand stone houses. Nowadays, these houses are tourist attractions.

The people who live in Jamaica speak English. They also speak what they call 'Jamaica talk'. This is a mixture of English and African words. Here are some Jamaica talk words and their meanings:

nyam	eat
boonoonoonoos	happiness and delight
talawah	strong and courageous
duppy	ghost

Jamaica was a British colony until 6th August, 1962. This was Independence Day when Jamaicans started to rule themselves.

The capital of this new country is Kingston. With its modern shops, offices, factories and streets full of traffic, Kingston is very different from the village of Cascade.